1969

2009

Lost Soldiers

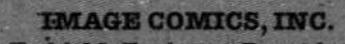

IMAGECOMICS.COM

LOST SOLDIERS. First printing. February 2021. Published by Image Comics, Inc. Office of publication: PO BOX 14457, Portland, OR 97293.

Printed in the USA. For international rights, contact: foreignlicensing@imagecomics.com.
ISBN: 978-1-5343-1820-5.

Aleš Kot Writer
Luca Casalanguida Artist
Heather Marie Lawrence Moore Color Artist
Aditya Bidikar Letterer
Tom Muller Designer
Ryan Brewer Production Artist

LOST SOLDIERS

LOST SOLDIERS

"The first act of violence that patriarchy demands of males is not violence toward women. Instead patriarchy demands of all males that they engage in acts of psychic self-mutilation, that they kill off the emotional parts of themselves. If an individual is not successful in emotionally crippling himself, he can count on patriarchal men to enact rituals of power that will assault his self-esteem."
—bell hooks,
"The Will to Change: Men, Masculinity, and Love"

"This is my home / This thin edge of / Barbwire"
—Gloria Evangelina Anzaldúa,
"Borderlands/La Frontera: The New Mestiza"

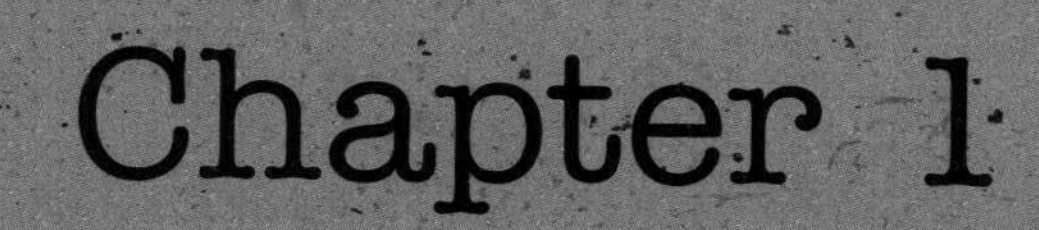

Chapter 1

IT NEVER LEAVES YOU, NOT REALLY

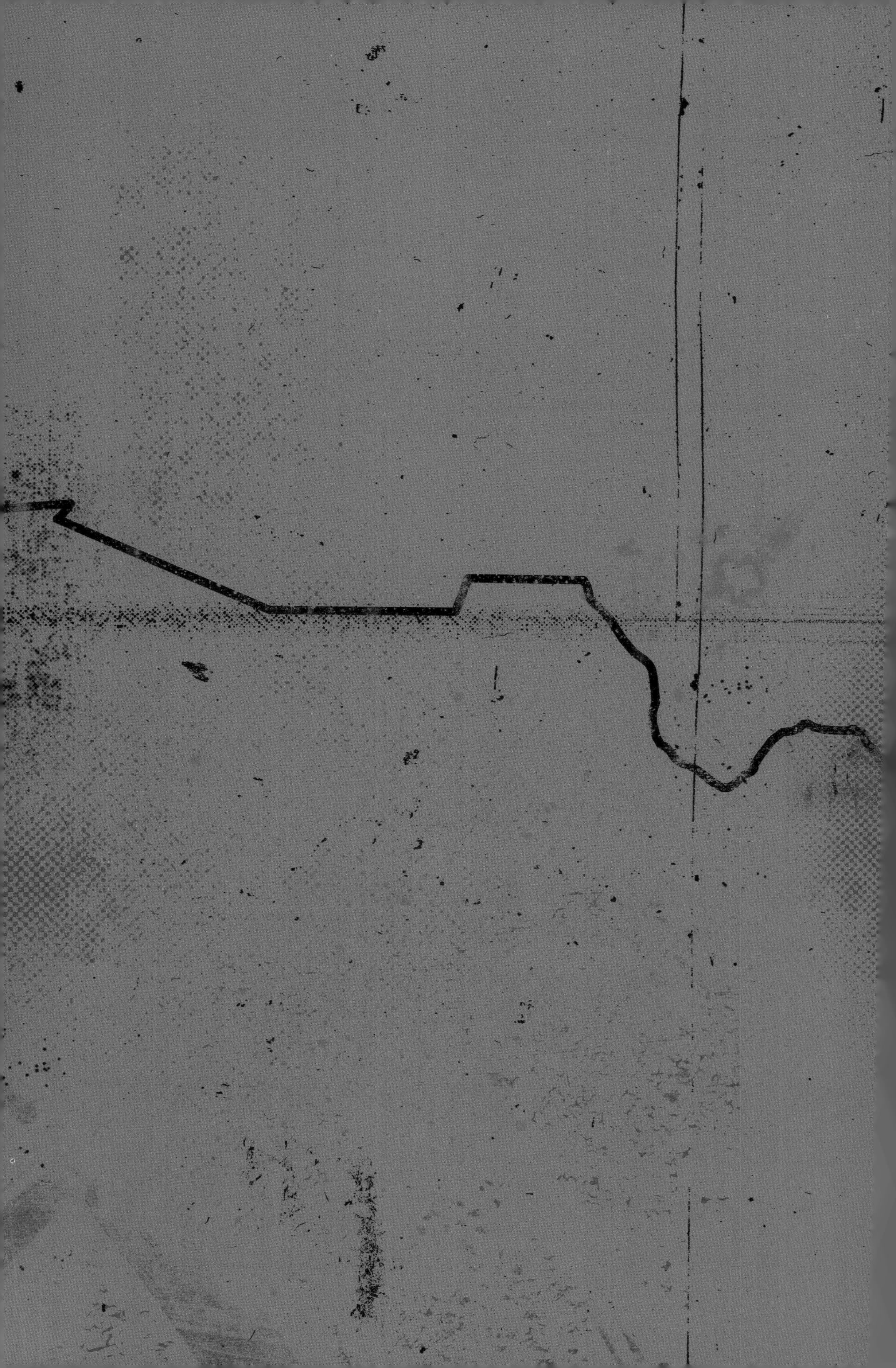

THERE'S MEMORY IN THE MUD.
TREMBLING BREATHS OF THE DEAD GRASPING TO HOLD ON TO WHAT IS ALREADY LOST.
THEY COME BURY WOMEN AND CHILDREN HERE. THEY RAPE THEM AND KILL THEM AND THEY BURY THEM HERE BECAUSE NOBODY CARES ABOUT THE DEAD BODIES OF WOMEN AND CHILDREN UNLESS THE WOMEN ARE JOURNALISTS OR THE CHILDREN STUDENTS WHO HAVE PROTESTED FOR TOO LONG.
THE BODIES OF MEN, THOSE BECOME EXPOSED IN THE BUSY STREETS, ACROSS THE EARLY MORNING BRIDGES, AN ARCHITECTURE OF PAIN, MORE BORDERS TO PUT FEAR IN OTHER MEN.
THE MEN SEE THE DEMARCATIONS. THEIR SHARP INHALES MERGE WITH THE INCOMPREHENSIBLE VOICES OF GHOSTS BEGGING FOR RELEASE WITH THEIR TRACHEAS SEVERED BY RAZORS AND KNIVES AND MACHETES AND RIPPED APART BY BULLETS. BODIES BREATHING BUT ALREADY DEAD. FROGS CUT OPEN.
YEARS LATER THE BOY SLICING THE FROG KILLS ANOTHER MAN IN THE JUNGLE.
NO.
WHAT HE DOES IS HE KILLS THE SOUL OF THE MAN BUT THE BODY LIVES ON.

THE SOUND OF A THROAT BEING OPENED LIKE A PLASTIC CURTAIN PACKED WITH BLOOD AND AIR POCKETS AND WRAPPED TIGHT. SLICE OVER IT HECTIC AND UNEVEN AND LIFE RELEASES IN A LONG BROKEN LINE OF FITS AND SPURTS.
SINCE 1976
FRESHLY ABANDONED HOUSES WITH FURNITURE STILL INSIDE, TELEPHONES WEEPING IN THE DESERT WIND.
THE FAMILIES ARE TALL SHADOWS VANISHING INTO THE DARK. CLOSE TO THEM AND FIRST TO BE EATEN BY THE VOID ARE THE SMALL BACKS OF THE CHILDREN.
THERE'S NO MERCIFUL SOUND TO DEFINE THE MOMENT WHEN A HUMAN BEING BECOMES A GHOST. NO ANNOUNCEMENT SO THAT THE WORLD CAN BE HELD TO ACCOUNT.
NOTHING BUT THE MEMORY OF THE MUD.

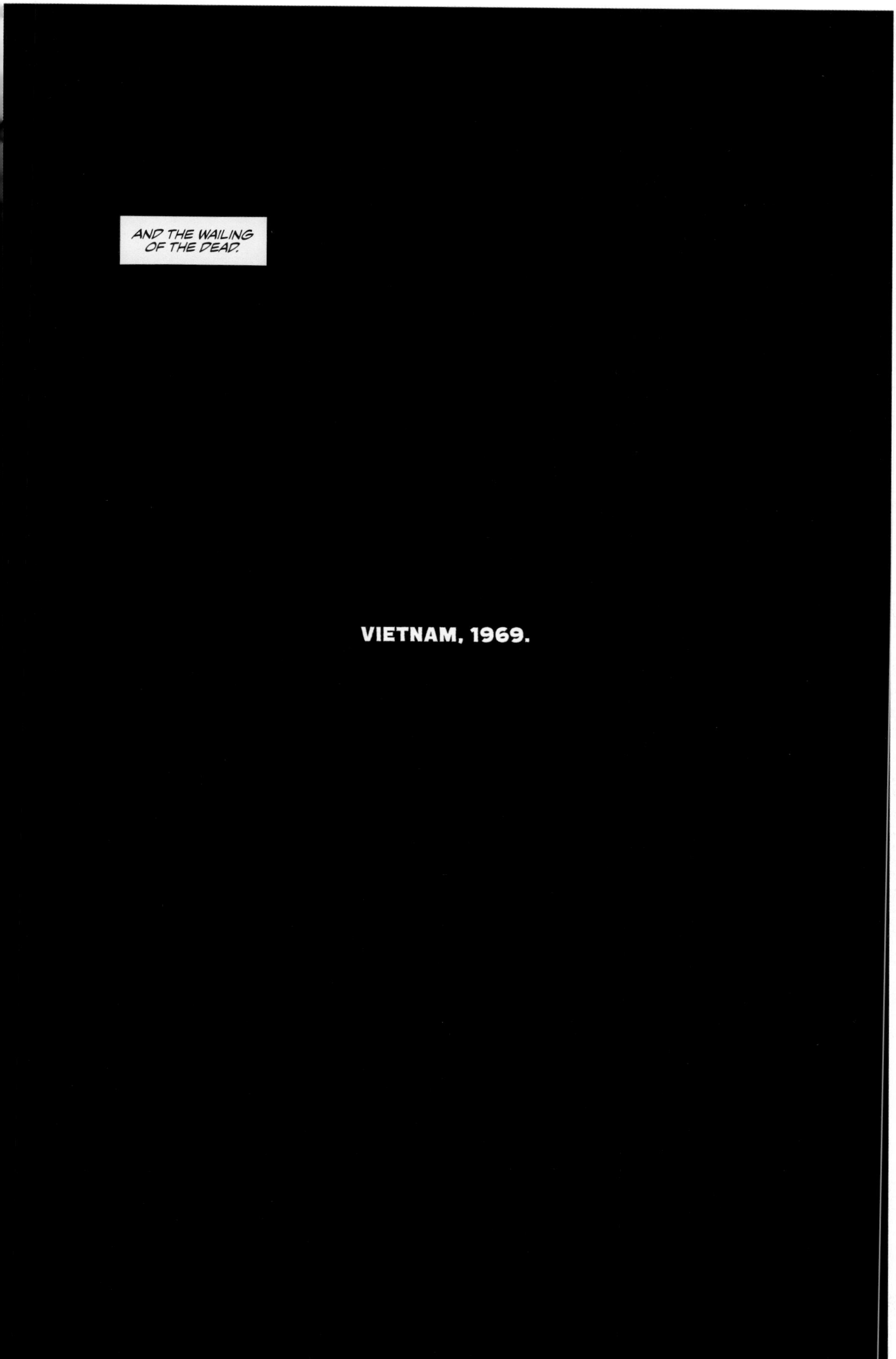

AND THE WAILING OF THE DEAD.

VIETNAM, 1969.

IF YOU'RE ASKING WHO THE ABSOLUTE NUMBER ONE HERO IS, I GOTTA GO WITH JOHN WAYNE, MAN. AIN'T NOBODY LIKE THE DUKE. COMES TO TOWN, CLEANS IT UP. DOESN'T COMPLAIN, DOESN'T WASTE TIME. YOU CAN RELY. INSPIRATIONAL.
SHOW ME A MAN WHO WOULDN'T LIKE THE DUKE TO SHOW UP IN THE DOOR WITH A DEAD GOOK ON THE TIP OF THE BAYONET AND A PLAN ON HOW TO END THE WAR IN FORTY-EIGHT HOURS AND I'LL SHOW YOU A MAN WHO--
SUPERMAN.
...WHAT?
CLARK KENT. SUPERMAN.
FIGURES, WHAT ELSE SHOULD I EXPECT FROM A JEW, OF COURSE IT'S A JEWISH SPACE HIPPIE JESUS...

YOU, SERGEANT KOWALSKI? WHO'S YOUR HERO?
BERG, HOW'S YOUR WATCH?
IT AIN'T BAD, SARGE. ALL QUIET ON THE ASIAN FRONT, AND HAWKINS IS DOING HIS BEST TO INTRODUCE ME TO THE FINE ART OF KNOWING JUST ABOUT EVERYTHING THERE IS TO KNOW ABOUT OUR SACRED DUTY TO BRING DEMOCRACY TO THE HEATHENS BY THE WAY OF MILITARY INTERVENTION AND POPULAR CULTURE.
HAWKINS. MAKE SURE YOU INTRODUCE BERG TO THE FINE ART OF WATCHING THE ASSES OF EVERYONE ON THIS HILL AND NOT RUNNING HIS MOUTH FOR TOO LONG.
YOU KEEP YOUR MOUTH OPEN FOR TOO LONG, BERG, VIETCONG BULLETS TEND TO FIND THEIR WAY IN. SAME GOES FOR PAYING ATTENTION TO THE WRONG THINGS. GOT IT?
YEAH.
GOOD. SITREP, HAWKINS?
WE GOT SOME LIGHT MOVEMENT THREE HOURS AGO IN THE TREES OVER THERE BUT IT MIGHT HAVE BEEN THE MOON PLAYING TRICKS AGAIN. MAIN BASE PERIMETER DEFINITELY SECURE. AND I GUESS THE PATROL YOUNG BERG HERE SEEMS TO BE A PART OF NOW IS TAKING A LOOK TOMORROW?
YEAH. THEY'RE LOW ON MEN SO I'M ADDING YOU.
OH MA--
ANY PROBLEMS?
...NAW, SIR.

WHAT A FUCKIN' JOYRIDE, THAT ONE.
BETTER THAN BURKE, FROM WHAT I'M HEARING?
...WHAT HAPPENED BETWEEN THOSE TWO?
TOMATO TO-MAH-TO. AT LEAST WITH BURKE, YOU FEEL LIKE NOTHING'S GONNA HAPPEN TO YOU. KOWALSKI...HE MIGHT MEAN WELL, MAN. HE'S EVEN EFFECTIVE DOWN THERE. BUT AT SOME POINT, YOU GOTTA ASK YOURSELF...DO I REALLY WANT A SNITCH WATCHING MY BACK? OR DO I PREFER THE GUY WHO EVEN THE VIETCONG TELL SCARY STORIES ABOUT IN THE DARK BEFORE THEY FALL ASLEEP IN THEIR FUCKIN' TUNNELS?
THAT'S A LONG AND UNCERTAIN STORY AND I'M NOT TELLING IT WHILE KOWALSKI MAKES HIS ROUNDS. FUCKER'S PRONE TO JUST APPEARING BEHIND YOUR BACK ALL OF A SUDDEN. SPOOKY SHIT.
...WHAT'D YOU MEAN BY CALLING SUPERMAN A JEW?
...YOU DON'T KNOW?
...WHAT?
GUYS WHO DREW HIM, MAN. THEY YOUR TRIBE.
...I THINK I'D KNOW ABOUT THAT.
...YEAH? YOU EVER LOOK AT THE NAMES OF THE PEOPLE MAKIN' THE FUNNY PAGES?
...SHIT.
HEE-HAW, MOTHERFUCKER. BLESSED BE THE PEOPLE.
...MAYBE THAT MEANS WHEN I GET BACK... I COULD, I DON'T KNOW. MAKE A STORY ABOUT... ALL THIS.
MAN...NOT TO DISPARAGE YOUR OBVIOUSLY DEEP AND LONG-NURTURED ARTISTIC AMBITIONS, BUT...

...I THINK EVERYONE'S GONNA BE PRETTY DEE-LIGHTED TO LEAVE THIS SHITHOLE BEHIND.

NO SOUND TO DEFINE THE MOMENT WHEN MEMORY GIVES IN. HOW CAN YOU REMEMBER WHAT IT SOUNDS LIKE WHEN YOU WERE NEVER REALLY THERE?

YOU COULD NOT BE THERE. IF YOU WERE THERE IT WOULD HAVE KILLED THE REST OF YOU.
YOU WERE NOT LISTENING. YOUR EYES WERE CLOSED EVEN AS THEY STAYED OPEN.
IT WAS THE ONLY WAY TO SURVIVE.

A HOT KNIFE STUCK INTO A WOUND, PULLING BACK AND FORTH. THERE IS A PAIN SO BRIGHT IT'S ALMOST A SMELL, AND A COLOR, PLAIN WHITE, WHEN IT COMES, BEFORE IT GOES, THE ONLY SOLACE. IT'S NOT A KNIFE BUT A MAN DOESN'T NEED A KNIFE TO DESTROY EVERYTHING.
(I DON'T WANT TO)

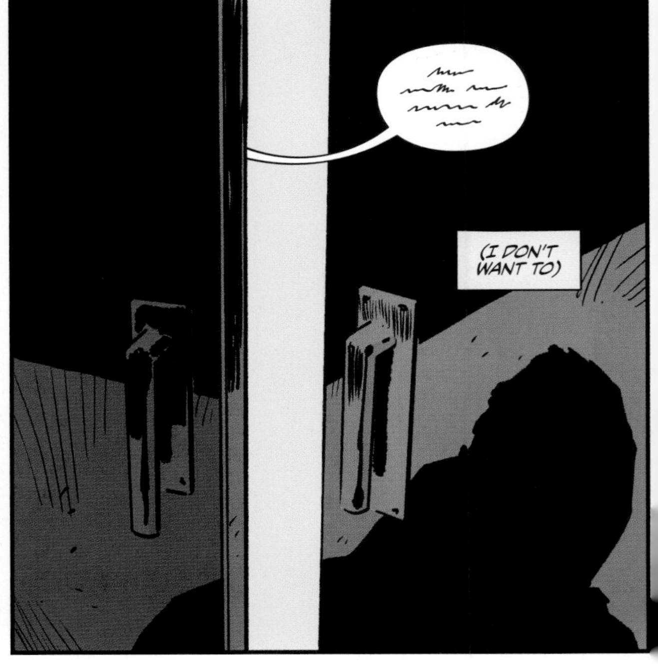
(I DON'T WANT TO)

AH, PERFECT, GLAD YOU COULD JOIN US, KOWALSKI. AS I WAS SAYING, TONIGHT'S A TWO-PARTER--ENGAGEMENT ON BOTH SIDES OF THE BORDER, SO MAKE SURE TO TAKE A GOOD DEEP SHIT, HIT YOUR CAFFEINE DRIP, DO WHATEVER THE FUCK YOU NEED TO DO TO STAY SHARP 'TIL IT'S MORNING SO WE CAN ALL GO HOME IN ONE PIECE.

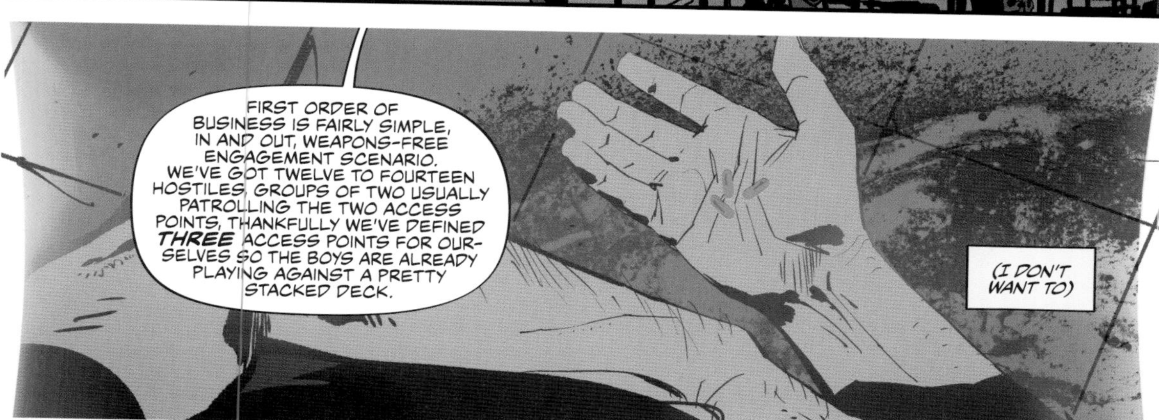
FIRST ORDER OF BUSINESS IS FAIRLY SIMPLE, IN AND OUT, WEAPONS-FREE ENGAGEMENT SCENARIO. WE'VE GOT TWELVE TO FOURTEEN HOSTILES, GROUPS OF TWO USUALLY PATROLLING THE TWO ACCESS POINTS, THANKFULLY WE'VE DEFINED ***THREE*** ACCESS POINTS FOR OURSELVES SO THE BOYS ARE ALREADY PLAYING AGAINST A PRETTY STACKED DECK.
(I DON'T WANT TO)

ANYWAY, THAT TAKES CARE OF ABOUT EIGHT TARGETS, THE REST IS USUALLY IN THE WAREHOUSE AND READY TO RECEIVE THE GOODS. THEY MIGHT TRY TO TORCH IT OR MOVE TOWARDS WHAT IS LIKELY A BASIC TUNNEL LEADING OUTSIDE THE PERIMETER--WE'VE DONE OUR RESEARCH AND THE DRONES ARE WORKING OVERTIME BUT WE HAVE NOT IDENTIFIED THE PRECISE BONE STRUCTURE OF THAT BIT, SO JUST LET THEM RUN IN THERE IF THE NEED BE AS LONG AS THE MATERIAL IS SECURE AND WE'LL PICK THEM OUT ONCE THE THERMAL LOCKS THEM IN OUTSIDE THE PERIMETER.

WE GO IN QUIET, WE GO IN FAST, SO THAT MEANS THREE GROUPS, LIGHT GEAR, SILENCERS, NO EXPLOSIONS, NO FUCKING NOISE. IMAGINE YOU'RE BACK AT YOUR PARENT'S HOUSE YOUNG DUMB AND FULL OF CUM AGAIN AND YOU'RE JERKING OFF ABOUT TO BLOW A LOAD AND IF YOU MAKE A NOISE YOUR ENTIRE FAMILY OPENS THE DOOR AND STARES AT YOU FOREVER.
IT WOULD BE LIKE THAT, EXCEPT IN THIS CASE, YOU'LL ALSO BE DEAD. SO DON'T MAKE NOISE.

WE LOAD EVERYTHING WE FIND, WE MOVE BACK HERE, DO THE DUMP, TAKE A TWENTY IF WE'RE LUCKY, AND GET MOVING AGAIN...

(I DON'T WANT TO)

...AND THIS TIME I'LL NEED JUST SIX OF YOU, SO WE'LL FIGURE OUT WHO THE BEST PEOPLE ARE AFTER WE GET BACK FROM PART ONE. THIS WILL BE AN EXCHANGE TYPE OF A SITUATION, SOME OF YOU HAVE ALREADY DONE THIS ONE WITH ME BEFORE, ALL OF YOU HAVE LIKELY DONE IT SOMEWHERE.

THIS WILL BE A WEAPONS HOLD SITUATION, AND I WOULD URGE THAT EVEN IF THE OTHER SIDE MOVES A BIT, YOU'LL STILL MAINTAIN WHAT I'D LIKE TO CALL RADICAL CALM AND ONLY SHOOT ABOUT A MILLISECOND BEFORE THEY DO, BECAUSE THIS DEAL IS IMPORTANT AND THEY ARE OUR FRIENDS, NOT OUR ENEMIES, OR MAYBE THEY ARE ENEMIES OF OUR ENEMIES, WHICH WOULD ALSO MAKE THEM OUR FRIENDS, YADDA YADDA YADDA...

ANYWAY, THIS ONE'S HAPPENING RIGHT OUTSIDE JUAREZ, 3:30AM SHARP.

WHICH MEANS WE'RE CROSSING THE BORDER...

...WHICH MEANS TRUST NO ONE, ESPECIALLY NOT THE FEDERALES. AS YOU PROBABLY KNOW, LA LINEA JUST MADE AN ALLIANCE WITH BARRIO AZTECA WHICH MEANS OUR FRIENDS ARE REASONABLY UPSET. IT ALSO MEANS OUR OTHER FRIENDS ARE HAPPY.

IT'S HARD TO PICK A SIDE WHEN YOU LOVE 'EM ALL SO MUCH, YOU KNOW?

BURNT FLESH AND CUT BONE SMELL THE SAME AND THE SCENT IS OF BURNT HAIR.
THE BLOOD IS COLD FACTORY METAL PRESSED ONTO YOUR TONGUE. THE JUNGLE IS HOT SWEAT OF COPULATION AND MURDER FOREVER INTERTWINED.
MEDIIIIIC! MEDIIIIC! BERG GOT HIT! SEND ME A FUCKING MEDIIIIC!
NOBODY WANTED TO BE IN THE JUNGLE AND LEAST OF ALL BERG. BUT NOW HE LIES IN YOUR ARMS. A LANCED ABSCESS FULL OF GUTS.
DO YOU UNDERSTAND THAT I BREAK THE YOUNG ONES FIRST?

HAWKINS! GET YOUR RIFLE AND RETURN FIRE! WE HAVE TO MOVE!
BERG NEEDS MEDIC, SIR!
BERG IS DEAD! GRAB YOUR FUCKING WEAPON!

FUCK.

STAFF SERGEANT BURKE, THEY'RE FLANKING US FROM BOTH SIDES! WE GOTTA PULL BACK AND CALL ARTILLERY ON THEIR SHIT!
BURKE!

WE PUSH THROUGH.
WE HAVE A WAY OUT! IF WE TRY TO PUSH WE ALL DIE OR WE'LL LOSE MOST OF OUR GUYS! WE CAN FALL BACK AND CALL THE ARTILLERY!

THIS IS FUCKING INSANE, BURKE!

WE PUSH THROUGH.
DO YOU UNDERSTAND WHAT I AM NOW?

WHICH SOUL DISAPPEARS FIRST? THE SOUL OF THE BOY, OR THE SOUL OF THE FIRST BOY THE BOY KILLS?
OPENED UP.
HOLLOWED OUT.
DO YOU UNDERSTAND WHAT YOU ARE NOW?
SO WHEN'S THE LAST TIME YOU GOT YOUR PROSTATE CHECKED?
HUH?
GOT ME ONE OF THOSE DOCTOR RECOMMENDATIONS. AIN'T TOO KEEN ON GOING ALL THAT DEEP IN, GOTTA TELL YA. NEVER KNOW WHAT YA MIGHT FIND OUT ABOUT YOURSELF.

BEEN BACK AT THIS FOR A WHILE NOW AND I STILL HAVEN'T SEEN YOUR FAMILY. HOW'S MINNIE?
SHE'S FINE. TOLD YOU. GOTTA KEEP THE WORK AND THE FAMILY SEPARATE.
OH SO US DRINKIN' ENOUGH PABST TO DROWN A SMALL CITY MAKE US JUST WORK NOW, BABY?
AIN'T WHAT I MEAN.

WHAT YOU MEAN, THEN? YOU MET MINE LIKE TEN TIMES. YOU COME OVER, YOU NEVER BRING THEM WITH YOU NOWADAYS. I GET MINNIE'S BUSY, BUT LIKE... COME THE HELL ON.
WE'VE BEEN HAVING SOME ISSUES.
YEAH, I KINDA GOT THAT.
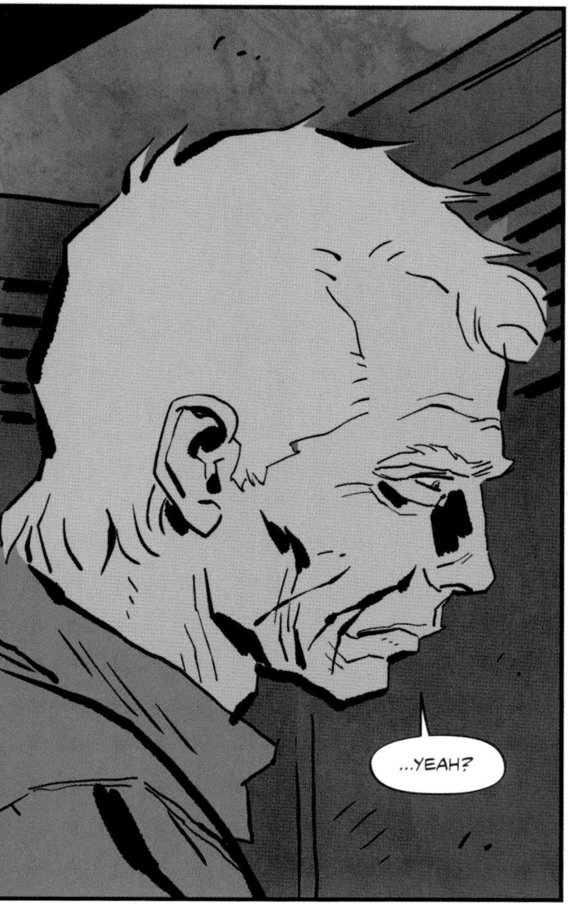
...YEAH?

YOU AIN'T EXACTLY HARD TO READ.
GONNA BE OKAY, THOUGH?
I DON'T KNOW.
I HOPE SO.

HOW'S THE ARTHRITIS?
AIN'T NO ARTHRITIS.
YOU UP FOR JUAREZ?
SANTO'S CALL.

I'M GONNA SIT IT OUT.
WHY, YOU SCARED?
WHY THE FUCK WOULDN'T I BE SCARED? IT'S JUAREZ, ASSHOLE.
HH.

YEAH, I'M GOING. DON'T THINK SANTO'S GONNA SAY NO.
YOU DOING THAT JUST TO FUCK WITH ME? BECAUSE YOU KNOW I'VE GOT THAT BROTHERLY IMPULSE AND I'M GONNA HAVE TO WATCH YOUR DUMB ASS?
THE ASS CAN WATCH ITSELF.

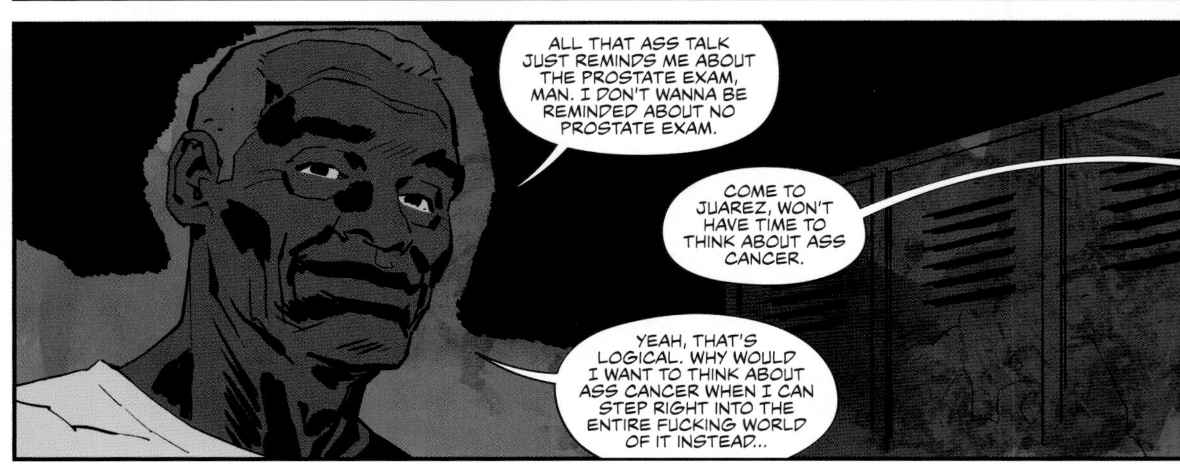
ALL THAT ASS TALK JUST REMINDS ME ABOUT THE PROSTATE EXAM, MAN. I DON'T WANNA BE REMINDED ABOUT NO PROSTATE EXAM.
COME TO JUAREZ, WON'T HAVE TIME TO THINK ABOUT ASS CANCER.
YEAH, THAT'S LOGICAL. WHY WOULD I WANT TO THINK ABOUT ASS CANCER WHEN I CAN STEP RIGHT INTO THE ENTIRE FUCKING WORLD OF IT INSTEAD...

SOLDIER. YOU OKAY?

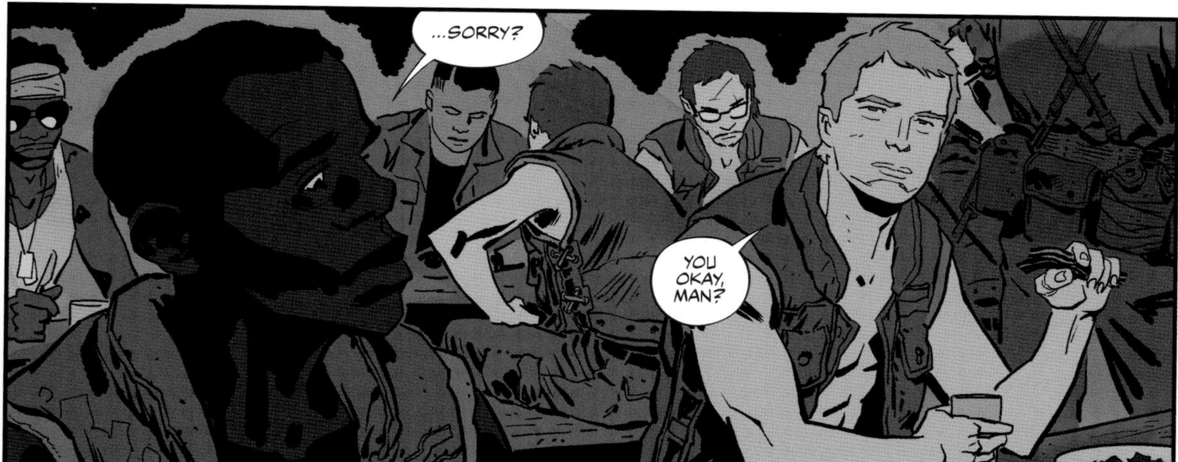
...SORRY?
YOU OKAY, MAN?

YEAH...NO.
I DON'T THINK I AM.

...YOU EAT ANYTHING?

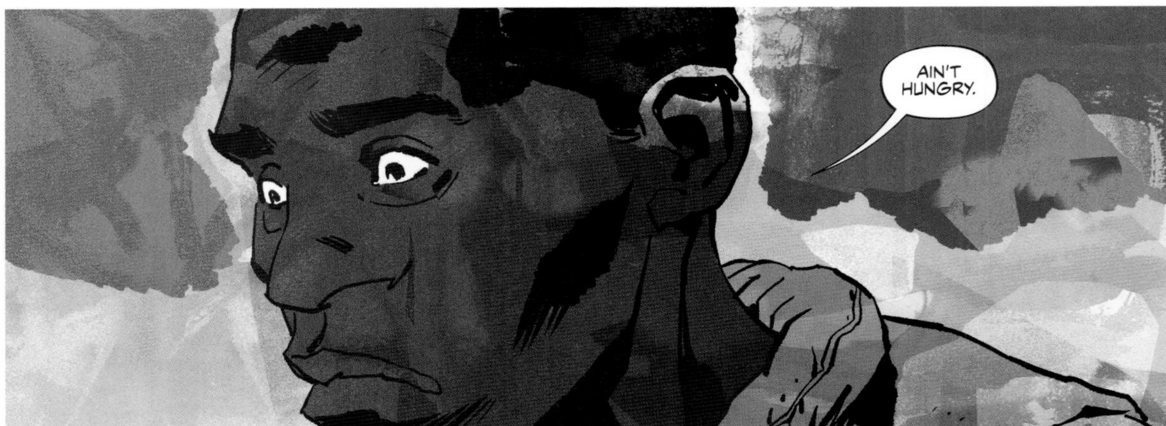
AIN'T HUNGRY.

AIN'T ABOUT HUNGER.
YOU GOTTA EAT TO SURVIVE RIGHT NOW SO YOU CAN SEE BURKE BURN IN HELL FOR GETTING BERG KILLED LATER ON. KEEP THE HATE COLD.

YOU EAT. I'M DONE. THEN GO GET YOUR OWN, TOO. YOU NEED IT.
WE WEREN'T SUPPOSED TO BE THERE. BURKE FUCKED UP. I'LL REPORT IT IN DUE TIME. THAT'S A PROMISE.

I NEVER LEAVE YOU, NOT REALLY.
SOLDIER. ANYTHING YOU WANT TO SAY TO ME?

NOTHIN' THAT WOULD MAKE ANYTHING BETTER. SO NO, I DON'T THINK SO.
MIGHT HELP YOU, AIRIN' IT OUT.

WHAT ABOUT YOU, BOY?

LET HIM BE. YOU'VE DONE ENOUGH.

HI, LOVE. I GUESS YOUR PHONE IS OFF, MAYBE YOU'RE ASLEEP OR SOMETHING.
WHATEVER THE CASE...
...I'M COMIN' HOME AFTER TONIGHT, I'M DONE WITH THIS THING.
I GUESS I SAID THAT BEFORE SO IT SERVES ME RIGHT YOU BEING ASLEEP RIGHT NOW AND ALL.
TREY DOESN'T KNOW YET...FIGURE I BREAK IT TO HIM AFTER THE SHIFT.
I MISS YOU AND THE KIDS.

I'M GONNA BE HOME SOON.
I AM THE PARASITE.
DO YOU THINK I AM DONE WITH YOU?

I NEVER COMPLETE.
MY GHOSTS WALK THE LANDS HOLLOW-EYED MUD-COATED MOUTHS WAILING FOREVER
MY GHOSTS COME WRAPPED IN FLAGS OF ALL SHAPE AND SIZE
I AM RAPE AND I AM WAR I AM THE BORDER AND I AM THE DOOR

YOU WHISTLIN'.
YEAH?
YEAH. YOU DON'T USUALLY DO THAT UNTIL WE'RE HEADED BACK.
JUST GOT A FEELING.
YEAH, WHAT'S THAT?
LIKE THINGS ARE GONNA CHANGE, YOU KNOW?

HEAR MY CALL

EXIT
JUAREZ
12
1 1/2 miles

34

LIKE THERE'S SOMETHING BETTER WAITING ON THE OTHER SIDE OF THIS.

White Killer in Juarez

Rumors of a death squad ran by a mysterious American operator lack firm proof.

THE INDEPENDENCE DAY MASSACRE AT ANEXO DE VIDA

More than 1800 executed in nine months as the cartel war escalates

What you need to understand is none of this would be happening without the Americans. Go back. Look at the border. Understand. The border is the invention that brings nothin but blood and pain. Was there ever a true border anywhere near Juarez? Why is it that Texas and California are the United States of America? Since when? This is all off the record, of course. I don't

CIA CATEGORICALLY DENIES INCURSIONS INTO MEXICAN TERRITORY

"CIA respects the laws and sovereignty of Mexico and its people" deputy John McMillan stated in a

Captain Martin, ~~you need to know~~ I don't know how to talk about this. But I have to write this letter in case anything happens to me or Hawkins. ~~The fact of the matter is~~ Burke ~~st~~ should have been relieved of duty a long time ago, and the

Soldier	You haven't got a clue.
Ian	What then?
Soldier	You never fucked a man before you killed him?
Ian	No.
Soldier	Or after?

—Sarah Kane,
Blasted

Chapter 2
IRREVERSIBLE

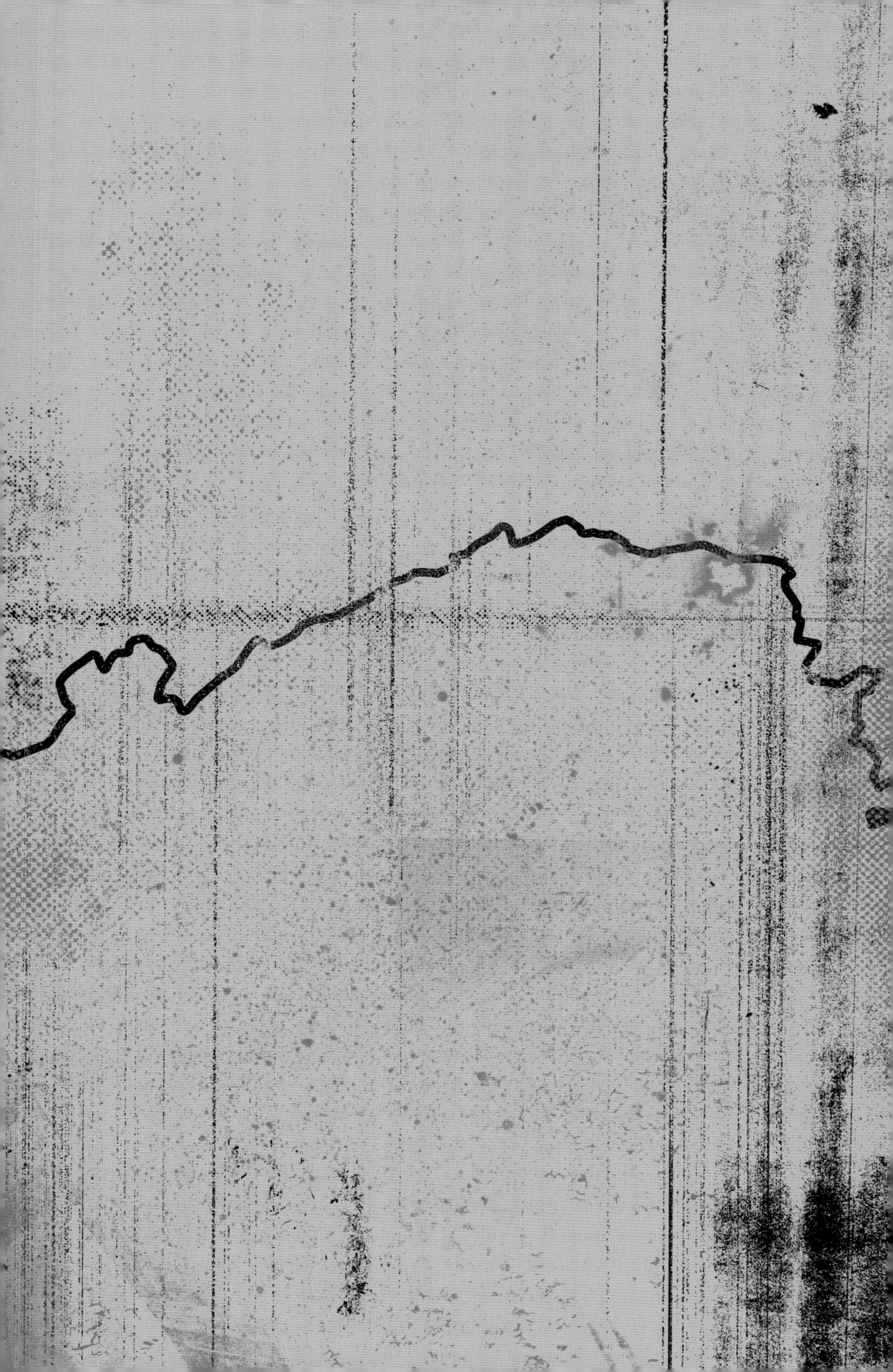

DON'T DO IT. DON'T DO IT.
THERE AIN'T NO GOOD IN IT. TODAY'S NOOOOT THE DAY.
FEEL THE LIVER EXPAND AND CONTRACT.

A LEAKY SINK.
A FAULTY PUMP.
OKAY. MOVE BACK.
WE REPORT TO THE BASE AND HAVE THE PLACE SHELLED. NO REASON TO TAKE A RISK.

DAMN. YOU'RE THE ONLY ONE WHO GOT SOME ACTION LATELY, BOSS.
DON'T PLAY WITH FIRE, GLASSER. KOWALSKI'S GONNA KNOCK YER TEETH OUT.
SHUT UP AND MOVE. WE AIN'T COVERED HERE.

IN THE FECUND HEAT OF THE JUNGLE IN THE PUTRID HEAT OF YOUR BODY A ROUND HOLE SQUIRTING PUS LIKE NAPALM.

THE MEAT OF THE LIVER CONTORTING ITS SHAPE TO EMBRACE A PIECE OF ITSELF NOW SEVEN FEET AWAY EMBEDDED BETWEEN METAL AND A PALM TREE. BREATH TORN AND SHALLOW THE SOUND OF A BLOOD RED SKY COUGHING OUT FIGHTER JETS.
NOBODY'S FILING A REPORT ABOUT THE FIGHT, HUH?
I DOUBT IT.
I DIDN'T ASK YOU TO DO IT.
YEAH, I KNOW.

WHAT DOES IT TAKE TO CURSE A PLACE?
FELT GOOD THOUGH, RIGHT?

HOW MANY UNMARKED GRAVES BEFORE I TOUCH YOUR NECK?
YOU'RE FUCKING CRAZY.

SOME MEN SAY I LINE THE STREETS WITH DOG CARCASSES ABANDONED CHILDREN'S SHOES BURSTS OF SOUND CARVING THE NIGHT. SOME MEN SAY I AM RESPONSIBLE.
AT NIGHT, WHEN THEY CAN'T SLEEP, I WHISPER BACK:
EXIT 22B
54 Patriot Frwy
Juárez | Ft Bliss
EXIT ONLY
Cruces
"NO. YOU ARE LINING THE STREETS FOR ME."

ANGELS OF DEATH. TANKS ROLLING THROUGH THE DESERT BREEZE. DAHLIAS IN THE WINDOWS INSIDE THE HOUSE A MOTHER SERVES POZOLE TO HER CHILDREN. IT SMELLS GOOD FOR A SECOND IT SMELLS ALMOST LIKE THEY DON'T BURY THE DEAD HERE ANYMORE.

THE STEW DRIPS ONTO THE WOODEN FLOOR ALL RED AND WHITE. LEAKING THROUGH THE TERMITE HOLES A FUTURE UNFOLDING IN THE SHAPE OF THE PAST.
SULTORIO MEDICO
CASE
TELEFONICA
INTERNET!
INTERNET
COPIAS
FAX

WHY WOULD YOU THINK A JUNGLE CARRIES LESS PAIN THAN A DESERT?

BURKE'S GONNA GO AFTER YOU.
KOFF

YEAH. GUESS HE MIGHT.

GOT ANYONE BACK HOME?
GOT A GIRL.
YEAH? WHAT'S HER NAME?
JOANNIE. GONNA MARRY HER.
DAMN, MAN. YOU GOT IT ALL FIGURED OUT.
WHAT ABOUT THE REST OF THE FAMILY?
LOOK. I'M GLAD YOU'RE GETTING OVER YOUR FRIEND DYING. BUT I AIN'T MUCH FOR TALKING. ESPECIALLY NOT ABOUT FAMILY.
KOFF KOFF KAHHFFF
FAMILY FUCKS YOU, MAN.

HEEURKKOFF
DAMN.
YOU OKAY, SARGE?
I'M FINE.
I CAN'T FUCKIN' BELIEVE THIS SHIT.

MEDIC!

NO CHILDREN OUT AFTER DARK. A PROCESSION MAKES ITS WAY THROUGH THE DEAD SILENT ARTERIES. TERRIFY A BODY LONG ENOUGH AND WHAT BLOOMS WITHIN IT IS A CANCER OF ONE SORT OR ANOTHER.
THE THING ABOUT SHOOTING A PERSON IS YOU PUNCH THE VOID INTO THEM WITH A BULLET.
A HOLE BLOOMS OPEN. WHERE THERE WAS SOMETHING YOU CREATED NOTHING.
OPPENHEIMER. INVADER.

I NEVER LEAVE YOU, NOT REALLY.
POLIC
GUESS IT'S TIME.
YEAH. GUESS IT IS.

WHO CURSED THIS BODY?

THE MAN DOESN'T KNOW WHERE HE IS. THE BOY INSIDE THE MAN REPEATS HE NEVER TOLD ANYONE. HE IS THINKING ABOUT IT AGAIN, DOESN'T WANT TO THINK ABOUT IT AGAIN.

IN HALLUCINATORY PATHWAYS HE REMEMBERS THE FACE OF THE MAN. HE KNOWS HE NEVER TOLD. HE SAYS HE WAS STRONG. HE SAYS HE BURIED IT AND THE MAN.

IT WAS THE ONLY WAY TO SURVIVE.

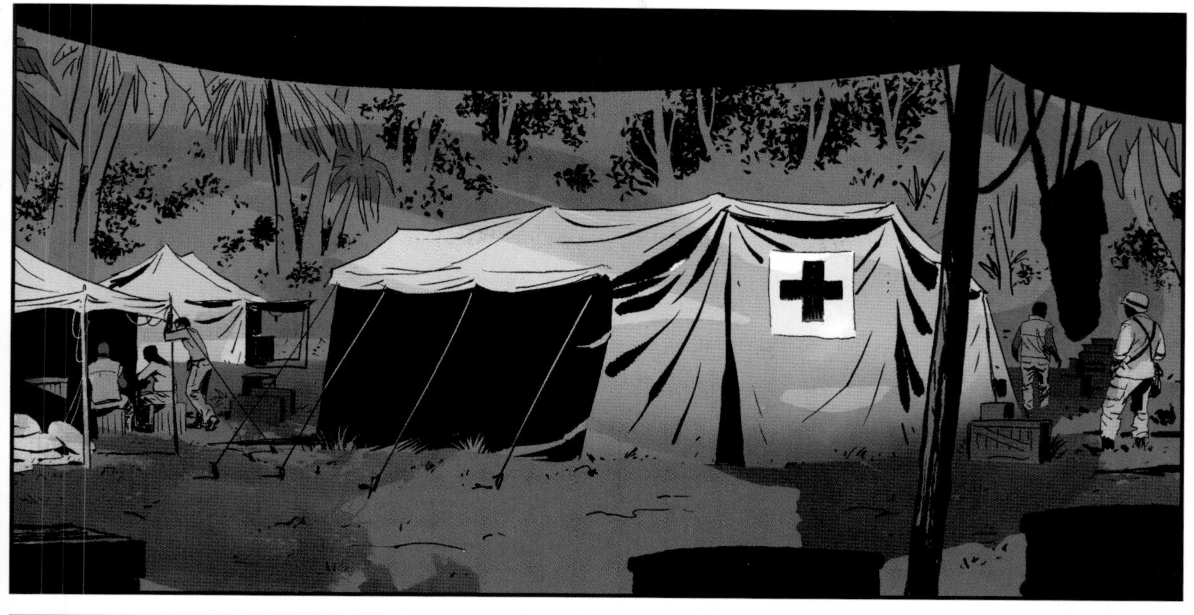

(I DON'T WANT TO)

(I DON'T WANT TO)
NO

THERE'S MEMORY IN THE BODY.
NO. YOU DON'T GET TO DO THAT ANYMORE. I'LL TELL DAD.

BUT HOW CAN YOU REMEMBER WHEN YOU WERE NEVER REALLY THERE?
I'LL TELL MOM AND DAD. NO. NO.

MAN. YOU'RE OKAY, KOWALSKI. YOU'RE HALLUCINATIN'. YOU'RE GONNA BE FINE.

JUST BAD DREAMS, MAN.
YOU COULD NOT BE THERE.

IT WOULD HAVE KILLED THE REST OF YOU.

I AM THE SYMPHONY OF YOUR FORGETTING.
ALL GOOD. LET'S BOUNCE.
DID YOU THINK I WAS DONE WITH YOU?

THE WORDS LIKE ROPES TIGHT AROUND YOUR GUTS. BILE INSIDE YOUR THROAT ALL THAT YOU HELD DOWN.
(NO)
HE HELD YOU DOWN.
THE HELL...

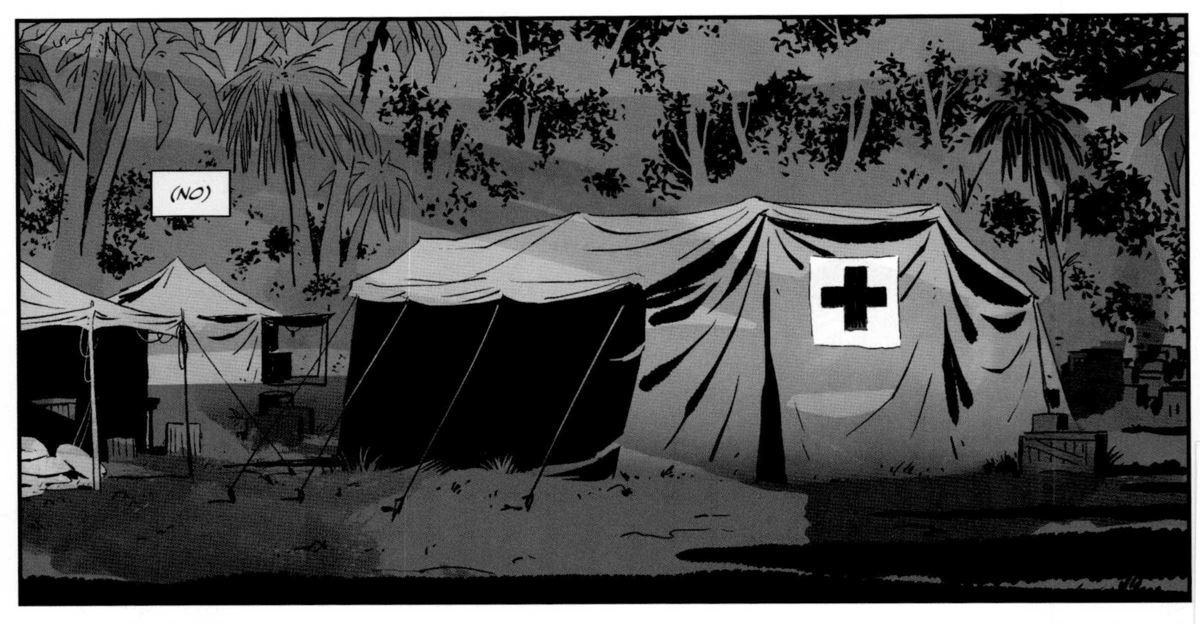
(NO)

(NO)

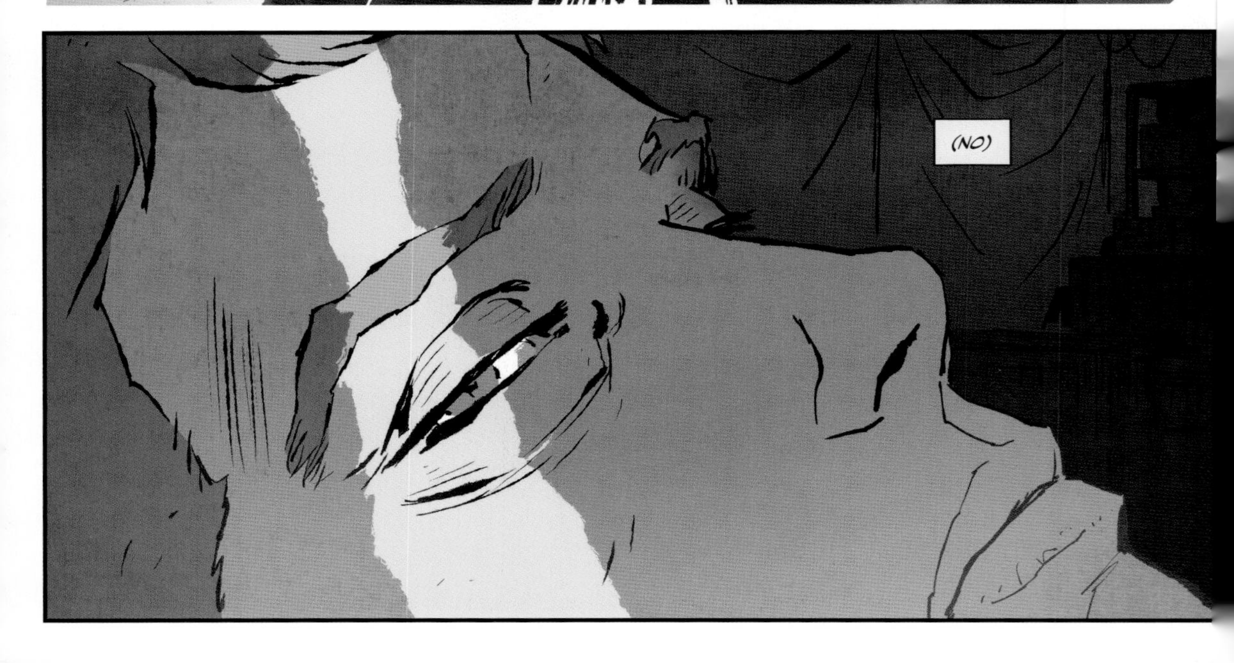
(NO)

...TREY?
(NO)

YOU SAID NO.

NO NO
NO NO
NO--
HRMM.
AND AS HE HELD YOU DOWN YOU BEHELD YOUR BODY FROM AFAR.
MOTHER-FUCKER.
AND AS HE HELD YOU DOWN YOU HEARD THE DEAD WAIL FOR RELEASE.

IN THE WAILING OF THE DEAD YOU RECOGNIZED YOUR OWN VOICE.

intelligence suggests

is willing to continue offering strategic cooperation in exchange for

permanent [REDACTED] [REDACTED]

in October 2007, asset S offered

confirmation of ability to influence stability of the region

asset X

placed within the circle

despite the uncertain agenda, [REDACTED]

[REDACTED] [REDACTED]

cc: [REDACTED]

group BIG MAN began its infiltration of group [REDACTED] in [REDACTED]

therefore placing asset X within the close circle could

"two sides" approach to

When the CIA re-approached potential asset BIG MAN, his rise to power

asset X

[REDACTED] [REDACTED] [REDACTED]

a strategic use of paramilitary and [REDACTED] groups

exchange

plausible deniability

"never really there"

cc: [REDACTED] [REDACTED]

DIRECTOR

12th December 2008,

a detainee in government custody provided additional data to suggest

to acknowledge the possibility asset X has gone rogue

[REDACTED]

he sides will likely engage in

via asset X, the leader of group BIG MAN expressed interest in becoming an asset if

shell shock noun

Definition of ***shell shock***
: post-traumatic stress disorder occurring under wartime conditions (as combat) that cause intense stress : BATTLE FATIGUE, COMBAT FATIGUE

In the receiving ward he found a patient shivering on his bunk with a diagnosis—in this case accurate—of severe ***shell shock****.*
—Albert E. Cowdrey

*A Veterans Administration psychiatrist, Dr. Jack Ewald, has reckoned that some 700,000 Vietnam veterans have suffered from various forms of "post-traumatic stress syndrome," the modern term for what was called "****shell shock****" in World War I and "battle fatigue" in World War II.*
—Stanley Karnow

combat fatigue noun

Definition of ***combat fatigue***
: post-traumatic stress disorder occurring under wartime conditions (such as combat) that cause intense stress : BATTLE FATIGUE, SHELL SHOCK

Nearly a half-million American soldiers were battle casualties during the fighting in Europe; by 1945 another 111,000 neuropsychiatric cases—then usually called ***combat fatigue****—had been treated.*
—Roger J. Spiller

The psychological strain he continues to endure has had many names over the years. In World War I, it was shell shock. In World War II, it was **combat fatigue**...
—Steven Lee Meyers

post-traumatic stress disorder noun

Definition of ***post-traumatic stress disorder***
: a psychological reaction occurring after experiencing a highly stressing event (such as wartime combat, physical violence, or a natural disaster) that is usually characterized by depression, anxiety, flashbacks, recurrent nightmares, and avoidance of reminders of the event—abbreviation PTSD—called also ***post-traumatic stress syndrome***

violence noun

vi·o·lence | \ vī-lən(t)s , vī-ə- \

Definition of **violence**

1a : the use of physical force so as to injure, abuse, damage, or destroy
b : an instance of violent treatment or procedure
2 : injury by or as if by distortion, infringement, or profanation : OUTRAGE
3a : intense, turbulent, or furious and often destructive action or force
the violence of the storm
b : vehement feeling or expression : FERVOR
also : an instance of such action or feeling
c : a clashing or jarring quality : DISCORDANCE
4 : undue alteration (as of wording or sense in editing a text)

---

war noun, often attributive

\ wȯr \

Definition of **war** (Entry 1 of 4)

1a(1) : a state of usually open and declared armed hostile conflict between states or nations
(2) : a period of such armed conflict
(3) : STATE OF WAR
b : the art or science of warfare
c(1) obsolete : weapons and equipment for war
(2) archaic : soldiers armed and equipped for war
2a : a state of hostility, conflict, or antagonism
b : a struggle or competition between opposing forces or for a particular end
a class war
a war against disease
c : VARIANCE, ODDS sense 2

[REDACTED] [REDACTED] suggest immediate

the list of disappearances likely attributed to [REDACTED], previously marked as [REDACTED], [REDACTED], or asset X:

Dear Mother
and father, it's trey.
you are probably
wondering why I didn't
write you so long
and

Mystery Man : We've met before, haven't we.
Fred Madison : I don't think so. Where was it you think we met?
Mystery Man : At your house. Don't you remember?
Fred Madison : No. No, I don't. Are you sure?
Mystery Man : Of course. As a matter of fact, I'm there right now.

—David Lynch and Barry Gifford,
Lost Highway

Chapter 3

SHELL SHOCK

WHEN A BODY FALLS FOR ME IT MAKES A SOUND AND THE SOUND IS THE SAME EVERY TIME.
THE BEAT OF DRUMS MADE OF TIN AND SKINS OF MEN. LOVE AT FIRST SIGHT.

THE RIFLES SCREAM METAL-LIKE UNDER THE ULULATING VOICES OF THE DEAD.
THE BRIGHT SMELL OF A GASOLINE TANK.
OF BURNT FLESH.
DO YOU UNDERSTAND WHAT YOU ARE NOW?

WHEN MY SONG GOES SILENT IT IS BECAUSE I AM FEEDING MYSELF.
NO.
GORGING.

HEAR MY DRUMS.
MEN'S EARS RINGING GOD-LIKE. AWESTRUCK BY THE NOTIONS OF CLARITY ONLY EXISTING AT THE END OF A RIFLE.

BANG THEM FOR ME, LITTLE BOYS.
BANG THE TIN DRUMS. TEAR THE OLD SKINS.

THE SKINS THE FLESH THEN THE BONE.
TEARING PAPER BAGS FILLED WITH AIR AND GUTS IN ONE LOUD CLAP OF YOUR HANDS.
HEAR MY DRUMS.

MOFLES
GARANTIA ES SU PREFERENCE

AND IF I AM SILENT

KNOW I AM CLAPPING MY HANDS IN HOLY CELEBRATION.

IF I AM
SILENT

IT IS BECAUSE I AM DANCING IN THE SPACE BETWEEN THE CRASH AND THE SCREAMING.

GHOSTS.

ALL I LEAVE BEHIND.

DON'T MOVE.
I SUCK ON MY FINGERS UNTIL THE MARROW'S OFF THE BONE.
THAT IS HOW I MAKE THE FLUTE.

YOU TOO FIRST HEARD IT AS A BOY.
WHERE DO THE BOYS GO

WHEN I AM DONE
WITH THEM?

OH

RIGHT IN THE
MUD. WHERE THE
OTHERS FLOAT.

I NEVER COMPLETE.
MY GHOSTS WALK THE LANDS HOLLOW-EYED MUD-COATED MOUTHS WAILING FOREVER
TWISTING TO THE RHYTHM OF MY INSTRUMENTS.

AND IF I GROW SILENT

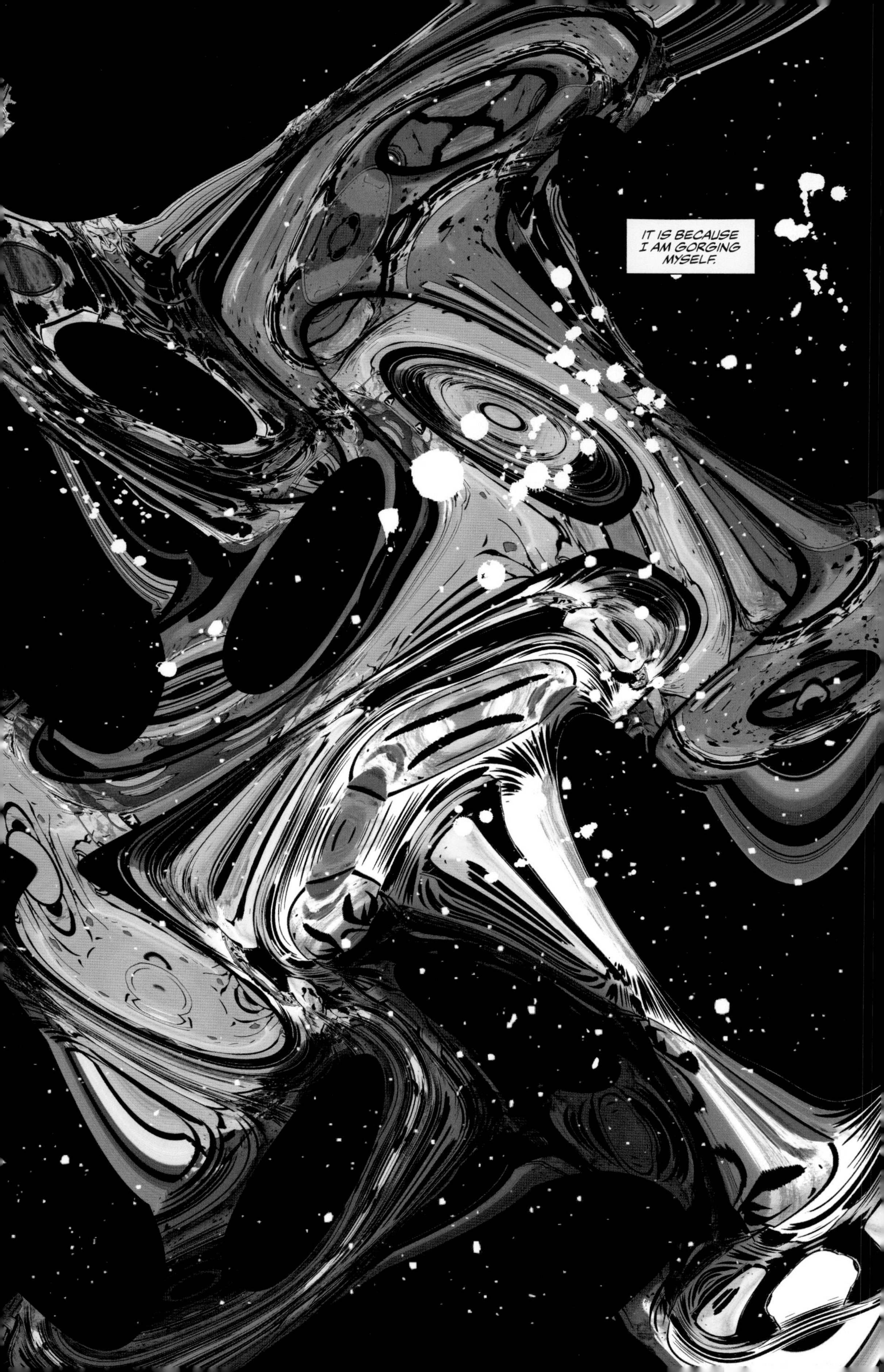
IT IS BECAUSE I AM GORGING MYSELF.

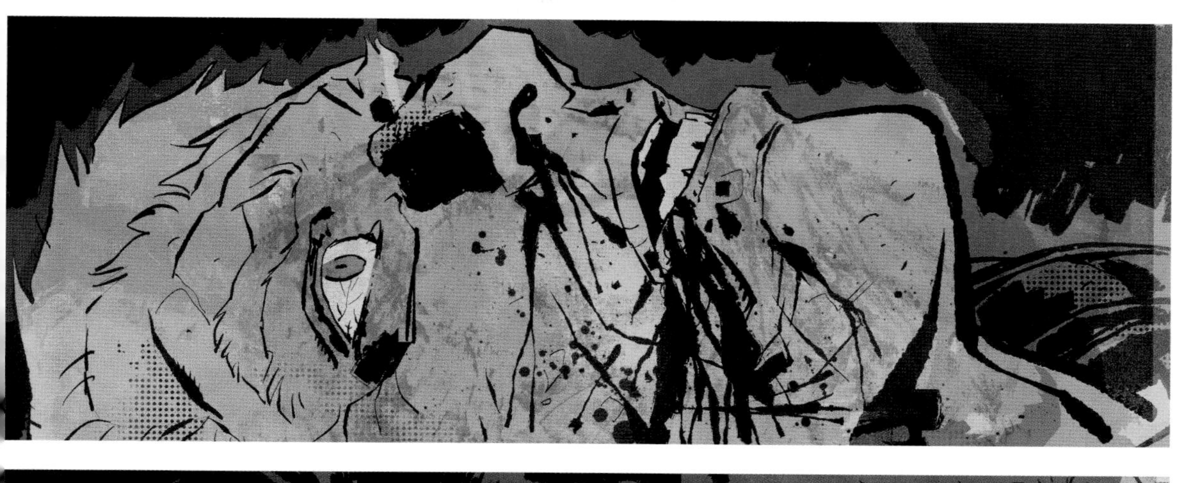

7651

8301
New Bay
MOTEL
JACUZZI ROOM
CABLE HBO
370

United States
of America
U.S.A.
Bienvenidos a Los
Estados Unidos
STOP HERE
IMMIGRATION
INSPECTION

HOUSTON
25 miles

Essa OIL
PICK N GO
Joe's STORE
STATE INSPECTIONS

SCHOOL BUS

Bud

WHERE ARE THEY?

SHE'S GONE.
I...WE...
SHE...

SHE JUST LEFT ONE DAY, WITH THE KIDS.
NOTHING I COULD DO. SHE WAS IN THE RIGHT.
ARE YOU REAL? I THOUGHT YOU DIED IN THE CAR. LOOKED LIKE HE GOT YOU.
I LOOK LIKE A FUCKIN' GHOST TO YOU?
NAH.
I WOKE UPSIDE DOWN IN A FUCKING ESCALADE INSIDE SOMEBODY'S HOUSE.
IF IT WASN'T FOR THE FAMILY I WOULD HAVE GOTTEN CAUGHT, BECAUSE MY BUDDY DECIDED HE GOT TO KILL THE GUY HE HAD BAD BLOOD WITH IN THE 'NAM AND JUST GAVE UP ON ME.
WHAT DID YOU DO?
BAD BLOOD. *HH.*
YOU KNOW HOW THERE'S JUST SOME THINGS CAN'T BE UNDONE?
...THAT'S THE KIND OF THINGS I DID, MAN. WHAT COMES AROUND, GOES AROUND, ALL THAT. I MEAN, THE FORM CHANGES, YOU KNOW, BUT THE PAIN, MAN, IT JUST STAYS THE EXACT SAME.

THE FUCK YOU TALKIN' ABOUT?
I...
...HOW LONG?

ABOUT HALF A YEAR AGO.
...SHE WANTED ME TO GO TO THERAPY, MAN. LIKE THAT WOULD HAVE...DONE SOMETHING. CHANGE THE PAST.
IT HELPS SOME PEOPLE.
BEEN HELPING ME FOR ABOUT THIRTEEN YEARS NOW...
WELL. YOU'VE ALWAYS BEEN A BIT OF A PUSSY.
BEER
...HE DEAD?
NO.
WHAT HAPPENED?
NO IDEA.
YOU MESSED UP BIG TIME, MAN. THEY PULLED US ALL BACK BECAUSE OF YOU. LOTS OF PEOPLE WITH LOST JOBS AND SHORT TEMPERS. NOT EVERYONE MADE IT OUT, YOU KNOW.
I FIGURED.
WHAT YOU GONNA DO ABOUT IT?
NOTHING.

YOU DON'T CARE IF YOU LIVE OR DIE? 'CAUSE YOU SURE SEEMED TO CARE ABOUT SOME-THING BACK WHEN I KNEW YOU--
I'M GOING TO GO BACK, AND I'M GOING TO KILL HIM.
IT'S THAT SIMPLE.
WHATEVER THE FUCK HE DID TO YOU BACK THEN, MAN. YOU WANNA HOLD ON TO THAT ALL YOUR LIFE?
YOU EVER HEAR ABOUT KARMA? I'M JUST A RUBBER BAND SNAPPING BACK.
YOU AIN'T FOOLIN' ANYBODY, MAN.
BUT YOU CAN CALL IT WHAT IT IS.

FATE.
NAH. A DIFFERENT WORD.
MATTER OF OPINION.
...YOU GONNA HELP ME KILL THE FUCK, OR WHAT?
THERE'S A PRICE ON YOUR HEAD ON BOTH SIDES OF THE BORDER. AND I GOT A FAMILY. I CAN'T, MAN.
YOU GONNA COLLECT AND GET OUT?
I'M GONNA KEEP TO MYSELF. AND I'M GONNA FORGET I EVER MET YOU.
I GET IT, MAN.
TIME DOESN'T REALLY EVER CHANGE, DID YOU KNOW THAT? IT'S JUST THE SAME STORY OVER AND OVER. WE ALL FIGHT IT, YOU KNOW? BUT IT DOESN'T CHANGE. IT'S JUST THE WINDOW DRESSING'S DIFFERENT. IT ALL BECOMES CLEARER ONCE YOU STOP FIGHTING IT, YOU KNOW? CAN YOU HEAR THE DRUMS, HAWKINS?
ANYWAY. I REALLY GET IT.

I DON'T HEAR NO DRUMS.
I'M SORRY I CAN'T HELP YOU, MAN.
IT'S FINE. IT'S MINE TO FINISH.
YOU COULD LET IT GO.
LET IT GO?
...LET IT GO WHEN?

KILLIN' A MAN NEVER MADE ANYONE MORE ALIVE.
YOU KNOW THAT'S A LIE.
IT WAS GOOD KNOWING YOU, MAN.
TREY. WAIT.

HELP ME.
I AIN'T IN THE REVENGE BUSINESS, MAN.
NEVER WANTED TO BE.

ME NEITHER, MAN.
BEER

ME NEITHER.

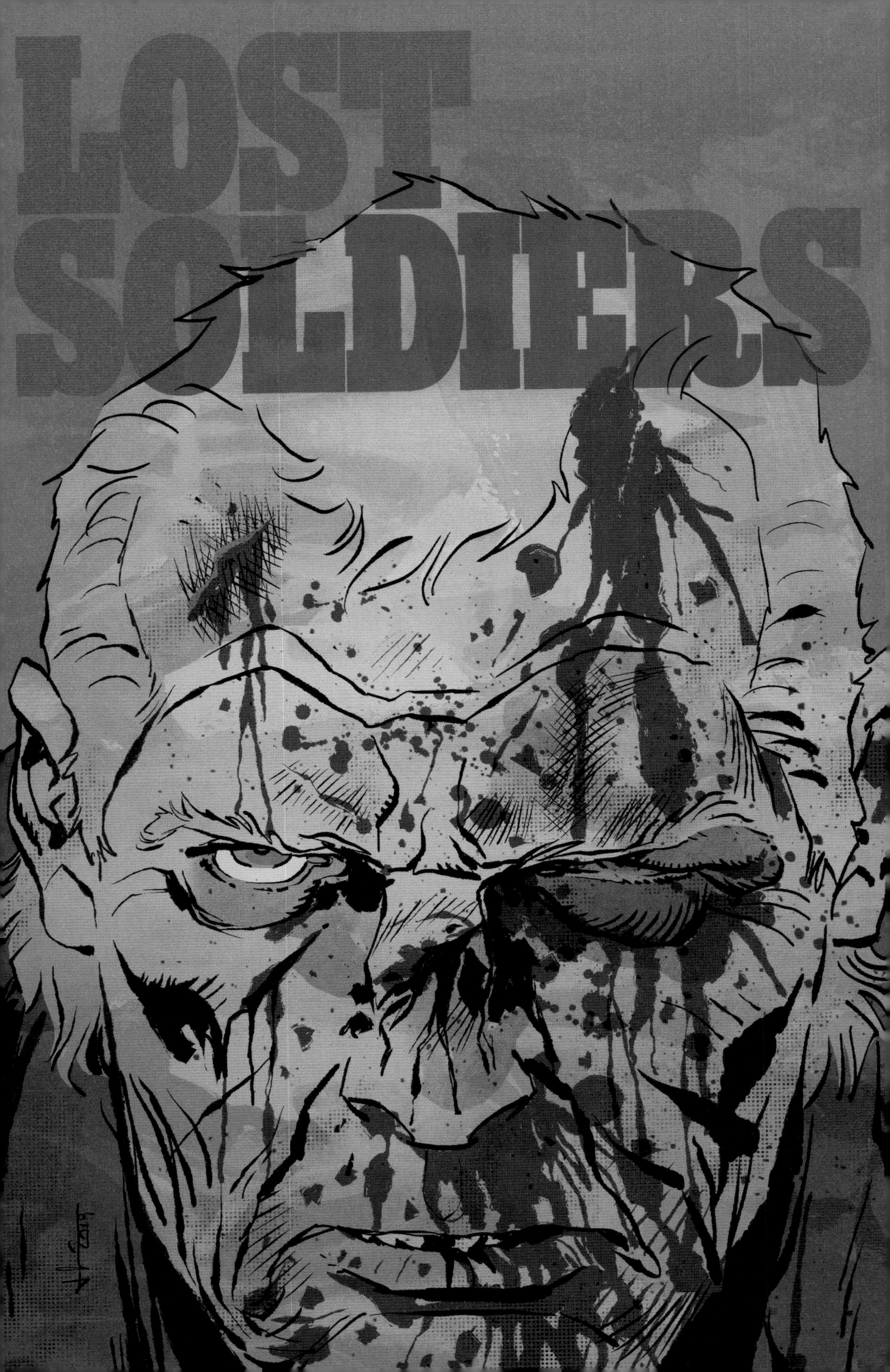
LOST
SOLDIERS

“They play, said the old man. Every week the anglos play a game to celebrate who they are. He stopped, raised his cane and fanned the air. One of them whacks it, then sets off like it was a trip around the world, to every one of the bases out there, you know the anglos have bases all over the world, right? Well the one who whacked it runs from one to the next while the others keep taking swings to distract their enemies, and if he doesn’t get caught he makes it home and his people welcome him with open arms and cheering.”

—Yuri Herrera,
Signs Preceding the End of the World

Chapter 4

PUNISHER

CHILDREN ARE SACRED IN THE EYES OF GOD.
<OH I DON'T THINK SO. NOT HOW WE WANT TO PLAY THAT.>

THE MEN WHO RECRUIT THEM TWIST THEM EARLY. AT ONE POINT I ASSUMED I HAVE AVOIDED SUCH FATE BUT LATELY I AM LEARNING I HAD NO SUCH LUCK.
<MAN, YOU'RE TALKING ABOUT GETTING TACOS LIKE YOU'RE SOME SORTA BOSS. YOU'RE SIXTEEN. YOU HAVEN'T GOTTEN YOUR ASS OUTSIDE YOUR VILLAGE BEFORE LAST YEAR.>
<SO YOU'RE GETTING TWO LENGUA, ONE POLLO, EXTRA GUACAMOLE, ONE COCA-COLA. I KNOW HOW MUCH IT COST, OKAY? SO DON'T FUCK ME.>
<OKAY, OKAY. GIMME THE MONEY THOUGH.>

<YOU KNOW WHAT? NO. YOU'RE BUYING. YOU'RE "ROOKIE.">
<OH, COME THE FUCK ON, JAVI...>
<DID I STUTTER?>

AT SOME POINT THE SOUL OF THE CHILD SOLIDIFIES INTO THAT OF A SOLDIER. THE HEART BECOMING A TIN DRUM. SOME DAYS I CAN HEAR ITS BEAT.
<THIS ISN'T HOW IT'S SUPPOSED TO BE.>
TACOS
<IT IS HOW IT IS.>

BAR AURORA
IT GOES LIKE THIS; BANG; BANG; BANG;
<FUCKING PIG. JOKE'S ON YOU.>
<PUSH ME SOME MORE AND I'M GONNA TELL YOU I FUCKED YOUR SISTER...>

BAR AURORA
BANG

ANYWAY. AS I SAID. CHILDREN ARE SACRED IN THE EYES OF GOD.

BUT THIS PLACE, WITH ITS SHIT AND FLIES AND OPENED BODIES? THIS CANCER OF A WORLD, PUSHING YOU THROUGH ITS NEVER-ENDING BIRTH CANAL, FROM ONE DEATH TO ANOTHER?
<FUCK FUCK FUCK>

NO GOD HERE.
JUST THE RIFLE AND THE C4 AND THE KNIVES AND THE WORLD OF HURT I DELIVER. PILING UP THE BODIES IN THIS CIRCUS OF BROKEN FLESH AND BONES UNTIL YOU HAVE NO CHOICE BUT TO COME.
KA-CHING

WHEN THE MEN MOVE ALL I SEE ARE SHADOWY FIGURES AS IF TREES TO BE CUT DOWN BY THE MOONLIGHT.
I AM THE AX AND I AM THE HAND THAT WIELDS IT.

IN THE CLEARING I MAKE WE'LL CONSUMMATE OUR FINAL UNION.
BANG BANG BANG

BAR AURORA
THERE'S A GANG WAR GOING ON. IT HELPS.
PRESS
JUAREZ.
I BAG THIRTY-SEVEN BODIES IN A WEEK. IT'S MY THIRD TOUR. AT THIS POINT, I'M FAIRLY CERTAIN THEY NOTICED.
SHIT, THE WHOLE WORLD NOTICED.
THE DAYS ARE HOT AS HELL. HUMID LIKE THE NAM.
RATAS
I LIKE IT. KEEPS ME IN TUNE.

IT. KEEPS
ME IN TUNE.
IN TUNE
KEEPS
IT
KEEPS ME IN
IN TUNE IT
KEEPS ME
IT KEEPS ME
IT KEEPS

MOTEL
SEEN TSUNAMI WAVES OF MEN AND WOMEN LAUNCH THEMSELVES AT AN ARMY BASE ONCE. BAD NIGHT.
NOT VERY DIFFERENT, THIS. ONLY BIG CHANGE IS I AM ALONE AND THE DAY ABLAZE WITH THE HUNGRY SUN. A MAN DOESN'T HAVE TO WAIT FOR THE EXPLOSIONS TO ILLUMINATE THE BODIES AND ENSURE HE HITS THE CORRECT ONES.
NOT SURE IF IT IS THE SUN OR THE PILING UP OF THE BODIES OR THE BOSSES GROWING IMPATIENT. WHATEVER IT IS THEY MAKE MORE MISTAKES, DELIVER MORE CANNON FODDER.
IT CAN'T BE TOO LONG NOW. THE BOSSES MUST BE MAKING SENSE OF THIS. I PAINT YOUR NAME ON THE WALLS IN THE BLOOD OF THE CARTEL MEN.
THE SUN ANNIHILATING EVERYTHING IN SIGHT. SAW A DOG THE OTHER DAY LOSING ITS BRAIN. GNAWING AT ITS OWN STOMACH GUTS BEGINNING TO SPILL OUT.
THE TV NEWS SAYS IT'S CALLED GLOBAL WARMING. ABOUT TO EAT US ALL ALIVE.

I SAY KEEP IT COMING.

BOSS SAYS IT'S TIME.

US
US

THIS IS ALL A LOOP, MAN.
BEEN HERE BEFORE, MAN. I REMEMBER YOU.
YOU'RE STUCK HERE WITH US. OR MAYBE WE'RE STUCK HERE WITH YOU.
WANT A SMOKE?
DON'T WORRY, MAN. THEY'RE COMING. THEY'RE ALMOST ON TOP OF YOU MAN, THEY'RE--

HERE.
PLATA MOTEL
POLICIA
NOW.

PLAZA MOT
<THE GRINGO REACHED OUT. SAYS "GIVE UP YOUR MAN, I HAVE NO QUARREL WITH YOU. IF YOU GIVE UP YOUR MAN I WILL CEASE ALL OPERATIONS.">
<I DID NOT HONOR HIM WITH AN ANSWER BECAUSE I TRUST YOU TO RESOLVE THIS BEFORE IT HURTS MY BUSINESS ANY FURTHER.>
<BURKE, TELL ME...>
<...WHAT DID YOU DO TO THIS MAN?>

IT'S TIME.

I SPENT DECADES THINKING THERE MUST BE ANOTHER WAY.

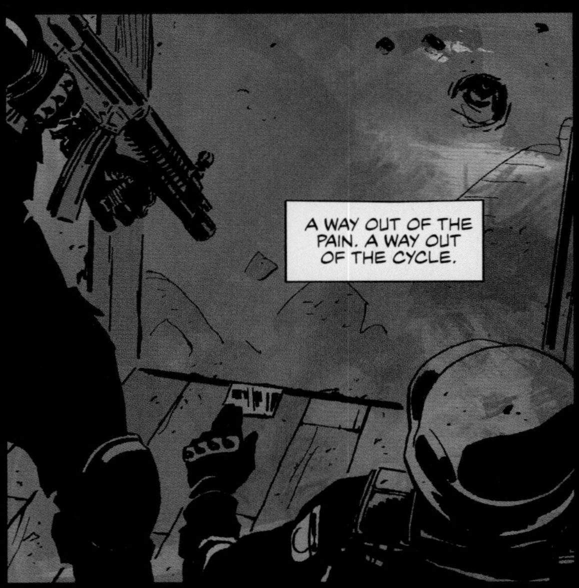
A WAY OUT OF THE PAIN. A WAY OUT OF THE CYCLE.

MAYBE FOR SOME OF US. MAYBE.

MAYBE FOR PEOPLE LIKE HAWKINS. THEY FIND SOMETHING, IT WORKS. LOVE, RELIGION, THERAPY. WHATEVER STICKS.

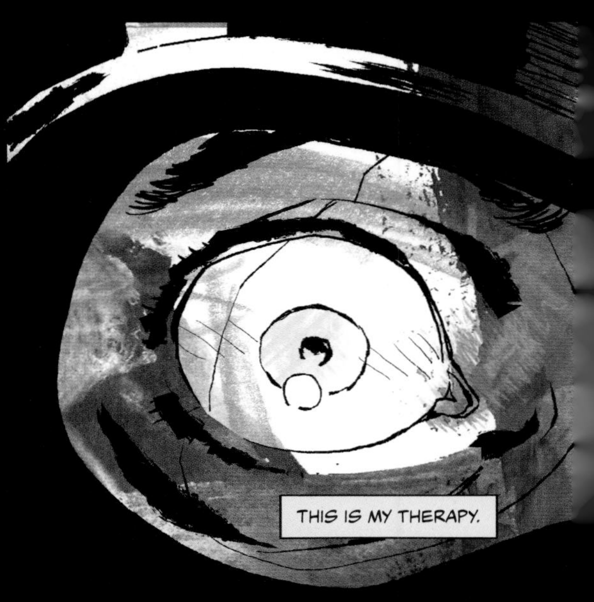
THIS IS MY THERAPY.

THE SESSION IS IN ORDER.

POLICIA

<MOVE!>
<MOVE! MOVE! I DON'T HAVE A CLEAR SHOT!>
<MOVE, MAN, I DON'T HAVE A CLEAR SHOT!>

<MAN! FUCK IT!>
CIA

CLICK
CHICK

PLATA MOTEL

HRRMM.

IT'S FINE. HAD ENOUGH OF A LIFE.
BUT YOU...
...I'LL OWN YOU FOREVER. LIVE INSIDE YOU.
YOU'RE NOTHING WITHOUT ME...
...I MADE YOU.

I HEAR THE TIN DRUM AGAIN. I KNOW WHAT TO DO.

BY THE TIME HE TURNS AND FIRES, I'M ALREADY UNLOADING THE RIFLE.

IN MY FINAL MOMENTS OUR EYES MEET AND I SEE THE CHILD I WAS ONCE. THE CHILD HE WAS ONCE, TOO.

BEFORE ALL THIS. BEFORE THE FIRST PAIN.

I REALIZE WE DON'T BELONG HERE. WE NEVER BELONGED HERE. NOT LIKE THIS.

ALL THE BORDERS WE MAKE FOR NOTHING.

THE LAST EMOTION I FEEL IS LOVE.

<OH SHIT.
OH, SHIT...>

<...WE GOT A LIVE ONE HERE, BOYS.>

LOST SOLDIERS

"After trauma the world is experienced with a different nervous system."

—Bessel A. van der Kolk,
The Body Keeps the Score: Brain, Mind, and Body in the Healing of Trauma

"Yes, and this is how you are a citizen: Come on. Let it go. Move on."

—Claudia Rankine,
Citizen: An American Lyric

Chapter 5

SEARCH AND RESCUE

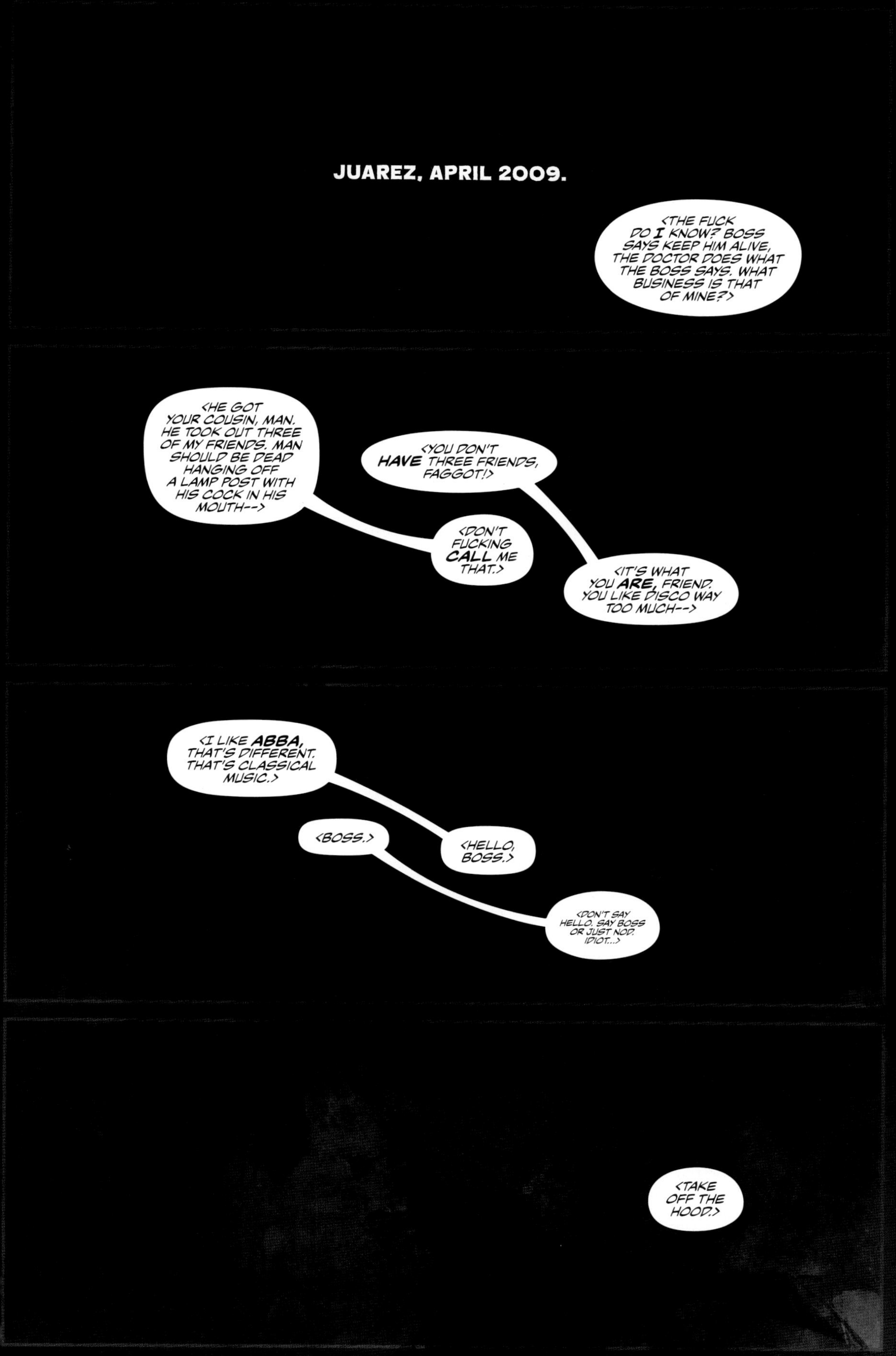

JUAREZ, APRIL 2009.

<THE FUCK DO **I** KNOW? BOSS SAYS KEEP HIM ALIVE, THE DOCTOR DOES WHAT THE BOSS SAYS. WHAT BUSINESS IS THAT OF MINE?>

<HE GOT YOUR COUSIN, MAN. HE TOOK OUT THREE OF MY FRIENDS. MAN SHOULD BE DEAD HANGING OFF A LAMP POST WITH HIS COCK IN HIS MOUTH-->

<YOU DON'T **HAVE** THREE FRIENDS, FAGGOT!>

<DON'T FUCKING **CALL** ME THAT.>

<IT'S WHAT YOU **ARE,** FRIEND. YOU LIKE DISCO WAY TOO MUCH-->

<I LIKE **ABBA,** THAT'S DIFFERENT. THAT'S CLASSICAL MUSIC.>

<HELLO, BOSS.>

<BOSS.>

<DON'T SAY HELLO. SAY BOSS OR JUST NOD. IDIOT...>

<TAKE OFF THE HOOD.>

HOUSTON,
NOVEMBER 2019.

I DON'T THINK IT EVER STOPS, REALLY.

I DON'T THINK THE PAIN... THE TRAUMA EVER GOES AWAY. NOT REALLY.
I THINK WHAT HAPPENS IS...I MEAN, I THINK I KNOW IT AT THIS POINT, I'M JUST INSECURE ABOUT IT, I THINK THAT'S PART OF THE TRAUMA SOMETIMES, TOO--THE WAY I UNDERSTAND IT, THE WAY A LOT OF THERAPISTS AND PEOPLE I...KNEW TALKED ABOUT IT, THE WAY WE TEND TO TALK ABOUT IT HERE, IS, I'LL NEVER BE THE PERSON I USED TO BE. AND I MEAN, THE THING IS, I'VE KNOWN THIS FOR WHAT? TWENTY, THIRTY YEARS NOW? IT ALWAYS RANG TRUE TO ME. THERE AIN'T NO GOING BACK.

GOOD AFTERNOON, MR. COWBOY.
I'M NOT A FUCKIN' COWBOY. NICE TAPESTRY YOU GOT THERE.
MHM?
THE PALM TREES. YOU GOT A PALM TREE TAPESTRY BEHIND YOU. I DIG IT.

WILD THING IS, WE DIDN'T EVEN KNOW WHAT THIS WAS UNTIL...THE SEVENTIES, DID WE? I MEAN, YEAH, WE HAD NAMES FOR IT. SHELLSHOCK, HYSTERIA, ALL THAT OTHER STUFF. BUT I DON'T KNOW. I MEAN, I REALLY LUCKED OUT BY MARRYING A CHILD PSYCHOLOGIST, I GOTTA TELL YOU THAT.
IT'S JUST... MOST OF US DON'T.
IT'S...IF WE TAUGHT EACH OTHER WHAT IT REALLY **MEANS** TO GO TO WAR. IF WE TAUGHT EACH OTHER HOW IT NEVER STOPS ONCE YOU BECOME A PART OF IT. HOW SOME FRIENDS COME HOME AND EAT A BULLET AND OTHERS NEVER STOP HEARING THINGS AND PISSING THEMSELVES AT NIGHT.
AND SOME OTHER PEOPLE...

WHAT INTERESTS ME IS, DO YOU FEEL BETTER?
YOU WANT SOMETHING.
TO SATISFY MY CURIOSITY, PERHAPS.
YOU KILLED MANY MEN. ON ALMOST EVERY SIDE. TO GET TO ONE. *WHY?*
NONE OF YOUR FUCKING BUSINESS.
EVEN IF IT SHOULD BE THE DIFFERENCE BETWEEN YOU LIVING AND DYING?
EVEN THEN. *COCKSUCKER.*

...GODDAMN, THEY JUST GET EATEN BY IT, AND THEN THEY BECOME ANOTHER... JUST MORE TEETH, ANOTHER HUNGRY MOUTH, AND ALL IT WANTS TO DO IS BITE AND EAT MORE PEOPLE ALIVE AND THAT'S ALL THEY'RE GOOD FOR FROM THAT POINT ON.
IT'S ALL THEIR RESPONSIBILITY. BUT I'VE SEEN EYES THAT WERE NO LONGER JUST THEIRS. SOMETHING ELSE WORMS ITS WAY IN. AND I, I, I DIDN'T WANT THAT TO HAPPEN TO ME.
I GOT LUCKY BECAUSE I MET THE RIGHT PEOPLE AT THE RIGHT TIME AND BECAUSE I DID THE WORK AND BECAUSE SO MANY THINGS CONSPIRED TO STILL HAVE ME HERE, FOR SOME GODDAMN REASON.
I GOT LUCKY BECAUSE SOMEHOW I DON'T HEAR OR SEE THINGS MOST OF THE TIME ANYMORE.
I GOT LUCKY BECAUSE SOMETIMES THESE DAYS THE NIGHTMARES FEEL MORE LIKE ONE MORE CHANCE TO SEE THE BUDDIES I CAN NEVER SEE AGAIN, UNLESS WE ALL END UP IN HELL, WHICH I THINK IS ABOUT THE ONLY PLACE WE'D DESERVE TO GO, BECAUSE WHAT WE DO, WHAT WE DID, IT ROTS YOU, IT ROTS YOU FROM THE INSIDE.
THAT'S WHY I STOPPED BEING A SOLDIER ABOUT TEN YEARS AGO.

I GUESS MY POINT IS, I WANT TO RECOGNIZE THAT SO MUCH OF MY RELATIVE HEALTH NOWADAYS IS LARGELY ABOUT MANAGEMENT.
THING IS, I'M ALSO A LIAR, AND I THINK THE LIES WE TELL EACH OTHER ARE THE WORST THING OF ALL, AND I THINK THOSE START WHEN WE LIE TO OURSELVES, AND I'VE LIED TO MYSELF FOR A REALLY LONG TIME AND I DON'T WANT TO ANYMORE.
MAYBE I'M GETTING OLD AND TIRED. MAYBE I'M GETTING WISE. I DON'T KNOW. PROBABLY JUST TIRED.
YEARS AGO, A FRIEND OF MINE ASKED ME IF I COULD HEAR IT. THE WAR. HE SAID HE COULD HEAR THE DRUMS, OR SOME-THING LIKE THAT. I MEAN, I DON'T REMEMBER EXACTLY HOW HE SAID IT ANYMORE, BUT I DO REMEMBER I KNEW EXACTLY WHAT HE MEANT IN THAT VERY MOMENT.
I TOLD HIM I DIDN'T HEAR A THING.

WANT A SMOKE?
I COULD HEAR THE DRUMS. SOMETIMES I STILL CAN. AND I DIDN'T TELL HIM.
I WAS TERRIFIED. I WAS TERRIFIED IF I SAID I DID, IF I ADMITTED IT TO MYSELF, I'D END UP THE SAME WAY HE DID. BUT THE FURTHER AWAY FROM THAT MOMENT I AM THE MORE I WONDER IF... IF I TOLD HIM...TELLING HIM COULD HAVE...I DON'T THINK HE DID WHAT THEY SAID HE DID. I DON'T THINK HE DID THAT.

YOU WANT ME TO WORK FOR YOU.
AND I THINK I FAILED HIM AND I WANT TO SAY THANK YOU TO YOU ALL FOR NOT FAILING ME.
I WOULDN'T HAVE MADE IT THIS FAR WITHOUT YOU.

'NAM. WE WERE NEVER THE SAME AFTER. WE WERE A COUNTRY ONCE. WE BEAT THE NAZIS. WE WERE A COUNTRY ONCE BUT WE WERE NEVER THE SAME AFTER. THE WHOLE COUNTRY DIED IN THE 'NAM.
HM.
YOU TELL YOURSELVES THIS STORY ABOUT VIETNAM, YES?
US

I THINK IT'S A THING YOU AMERICANS LIKE TO DO. TO FIND THE MISTAKE THAT CAN BE FORGIVEN, FORGOTTEN. PERHAPS EVEN UNDONE. YOU FIND THE *"FEEL-GOOD STORY."* YOU FLATTEN THE TRUTH, MAKE YOURSELVES LOOK LESS BAD. WE DO THAT HERE TOO. BUT WE ARE NOT AN INDUSTRY OF SELF-DELUSION. THE STORY OF VIETNAM IS, THIS IS WHERE YOU WENT WRONG AS A NATION. AND YOU REPEAT THIS STORY LOUDER AND THE LOUDER THE STORY GETS THE MORE AMERICAN IT IS AND THE MORE YOU BELIEVE THAT THE STORY YOU HAVE CREATED IS THE TRUTH.
AND WE WOULDN'T HAVE MADE IT THIS FAR WITHOUT YOU, BROTHER.
HEAR HEAR.
HEAR HEAR.
AND THE TRUTH NEVER MENTIONS THE ROOTS OF YOUR COUNTRY.
"ALL RIGHT, EVERYONE. YOU KNOW WHAT TIME IT IS."

YOU DO NOT MENTION THAT EVERY BORDER YOU DRAW IS MADE OF BLOOD.
...YOU DONE?

I DID WHAT I HAD TO DO. I WON'T WORK FOR YOU.
I'M A GOOD MAN. AND I DID MY GODDAMN BEST.

YOU KILLED YOUR WIFE AND CHILDREN. YOU DUG HOLES IN YOUR BACKYARD AND PUT THEM THERE.
YOU ARE AN AMERICAN.

YES, THEY DISCOVERED THEM. SO EVERYBODY IN YOUR COUNTRY KNOWS WHAT YOU REALLY ARE NOW.
THESE ARE THE CONSEQUENCES OF YOUR ACTIONS.
SORRY ABOUT THE MESS. YOU OKAY, TREY?

...IT REALLY NEVER ENDS, DOES IT?
129

OPINIONS VARY.
...AND BY THE WAY, MAN. FUCK JOHN WAYNE.

HH. YEAH.

FUCK JOHN WAYNE.